EASIEST KEYBOARD COLLECTION

Jazz Classics

WISE PUBLICATIONS
London/New York/Paris/Sydney/Copenhagen/Madrid

Exclusive Distributors:

Music Sales Limited
8/9 Frith Street,
London W1V 5TZ, England.

Music Sales Pty Limited
120 Rothschild Avenue,
Rosebery, NSW 2018,
Australia.

Order No. AM952061
ISBN 0-7119-7138-2
This book © Copyright 1998 by Wise Publications

Book design by Chloë Alexander
Compiled by Peter Evans
Music arranged by Derek Jones
Music processed by Paul Ewers Music Design

Printed in the United Kingdom by
Caligraving Limited, Thetford, Norfolk.

Photographs courtesy of:
Image Bank

Your Guarantee of Quality
As publishers, we strive to produce every book to the highest
commercial standards.
The music has been freshly engraved and the book has been carefully
designed to minimise awkward page turns and to make playing from
it a real pleasure.
Particular care has been given to specifying acid-free, neutral-sized
paper made from pulps which have not been elemental chlorine
bleached. This pulp is from farmed sustainable forests and was
produced with special regard for the environment.
Throughout, the printing and binding have been planned to ensure
a sturdy, attractive publication which should give years of enjoyment.
If your copy fails to meet our high standards, please inform us and
we will gladly replace it.

Music Sales' complete catalogue describes thousands of titles and is
available in full colour sections by subject, direct from Music Sales
Limited. Please state your areas of interest and send a cheque/postal
order for £1.50 for postage to: Music Sales Limited, Newmarket Road,
Bury St. Edmunds, Suffolk IP33 3YB.

Visit the Internet Music Shop at
http://www.musicsales.co.uk

Contents

ALRIGHT, OKAY, YOU WIN

Words & Music by Sid Wyche & Mayme Watts

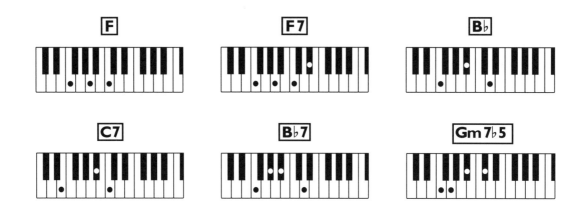

Voice: **Trumpet**

Rhythm: **Cool**

Tempo: ♩ = 108

Well, al - right,_____ o - kay,_____

_____ you win,_____ I'm in love with you._____ Well, al - right,

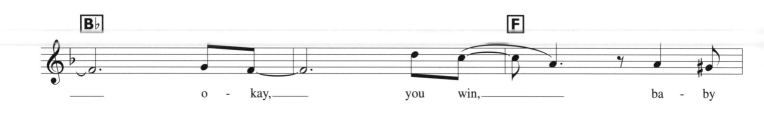

_____ o - kay,_____ you win,_____ ba - by

what can I do?_____ I'll_____ do a - ny - thing_____ you say,

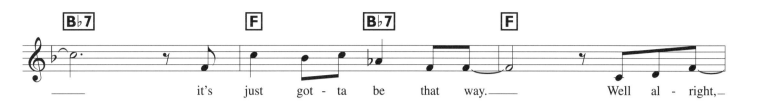

it's just got -ta be that way._____ Well al - right,_____

o - kay,_____ you win,_____ I'm in

love with you._____ Well, al - right,_____ o - kay,_____ you win,__

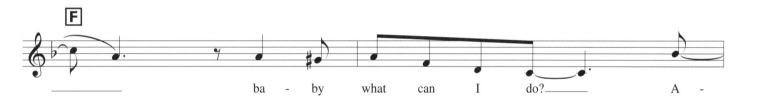

_____ ba - by what can I do?_____ A -

- ny - thing you say_____ I'll do._____ Sweet ba -

_____ by take me by the hand._____ Well, al - right,_____ o - kay,_____

_____ you win._____

AMERICAN PATROL

Composed by F.W. Meacham
© Copyright 1998 Dorsey Brothers Music Limited, 8/9 Frith Street, London W1.
All Rights Reserved. International Copyright Secured.

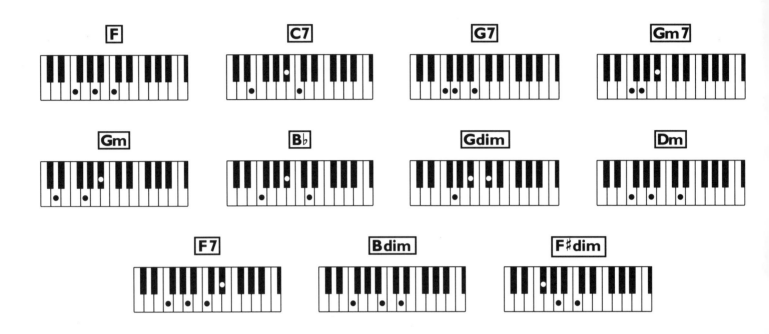

Voice: **Saxophone**

Rhythm: **Big band**

Tempo: ♩ = 108

BABY WON'T YOU PLEASE COME HOME

Words & Music by Charles Warfield & Clarence Williams

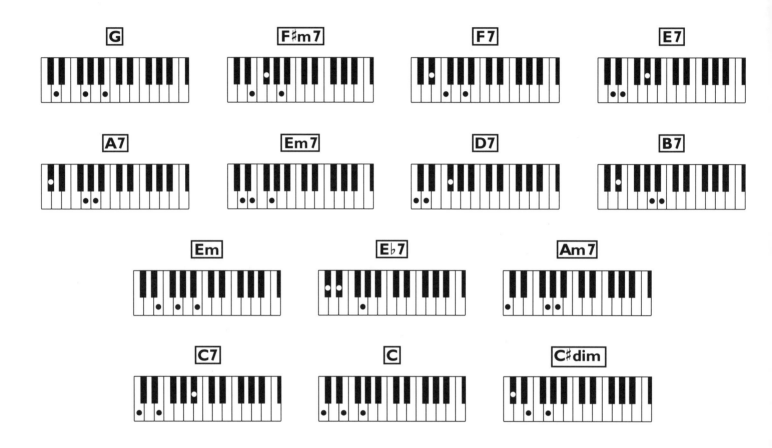

Voice: **Trumpet**

Rhythm: **2 beat**

Tempo: ♩ **= 96**

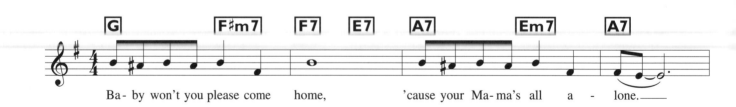

Ba- by won't you please come home, 'cause your Ma- ma's all a - lone.

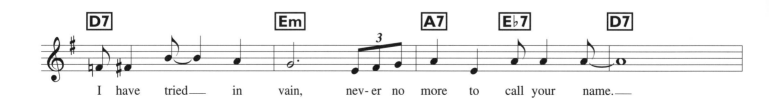

I have tried in vain, nev- er no more to call your name.

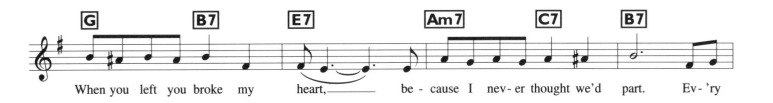

When you left you broke my heart,_____ be - cause I nev - er thought we'd part. Ev - 'ry

hour in the day—— you will hear me say,—— ba - by won't you please come home.

Ba - by won't you please come home, 'cause your Ma - ma's all a - lone._____

I have tried—— in vain, nev - er no more to call your name.——

When you left you broke my heart,_____ be - cause I nev - er thought we'd part. Ev - 'ry

hour in the day—— you will hear me say,—— ba - by won't you please come

home, Dad - dy needs Ma - ma, Ba - by won't you please come home.——

BOOGIE WOOGIE BUGLE BOY

Words & Music by Don Raye & Hughie Prince

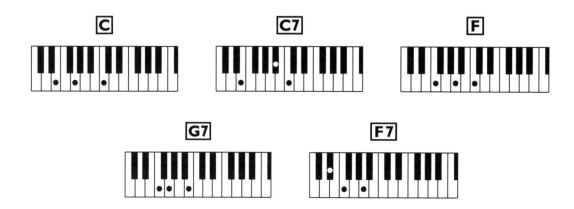

Voice: **Trumpet**

Rhythm: **Cool**

Tempo: ♩ = 112

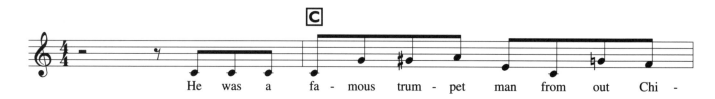

He was a fa - mous trum - pet man from out Chi -

- ca - go way,___ he had a "boo - gie" style that no one

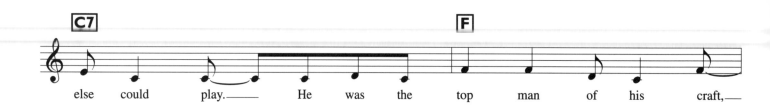

else could play.___ He was the top man of his craft,___

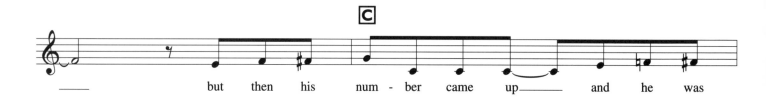

___ but then his num - ber came up___ and he was

gone with the draft.___ He's in the ar - my now a - blow - in' re - veil - le, he's the

boo - gie woo - gie bu - gle boy of com - pa - ny B.___ They

made him blow a bu - gle for his Un - cle Sam,___ it

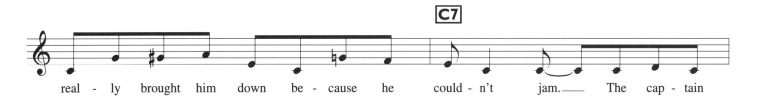

real - ly brought him down be - cause he could - n't jam.___ The cap - tain

seemed to un - der - stand___ be - cause the next day the "cap"___ went out and

draft - ed a band. And now the comp - 'ny jumps when he plays re - veil - le, he's the

boo - gie woo - gie bu - gle boy of com - pa - ny B.___

CUTE

Words by Stanley Styne
Music by Neal Hefti

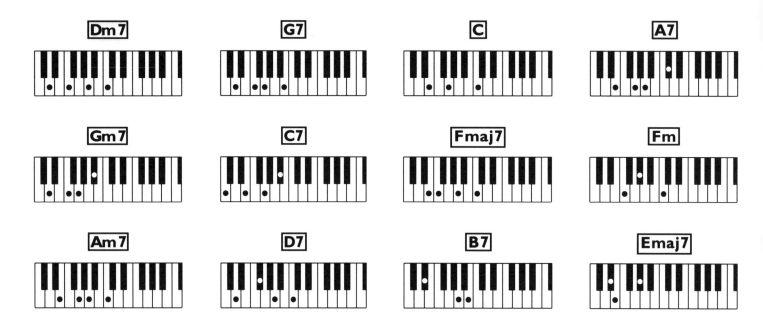

Voice: **Clarinet**

Rhythm: **2 beat**

Tempo: ♩ = 126

Mind if I say you're cute!___

In ev - 'ry way you're cute!___

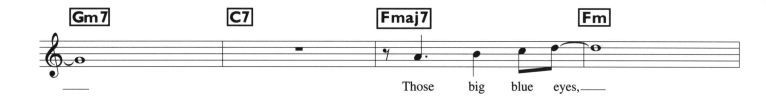

___ Those big blue eyes,___

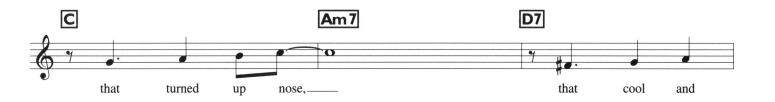

that turned up nose, _____ that cool and

care - free pose. _____

I mean I like your style. _____

That sly in - tri - guing smile. _____

_____ Your ev - 'ry mood, _____

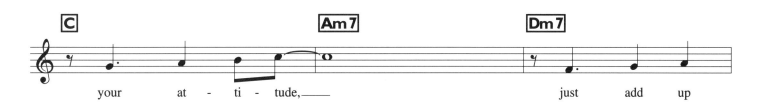

your at - ti - tude, _____ just add up

to you're cute. _____

DON'T DREAM OF ANYBODY BUT ME
(Li'l Darlin')

Words by Bart Howard
Music by Neal Hefti

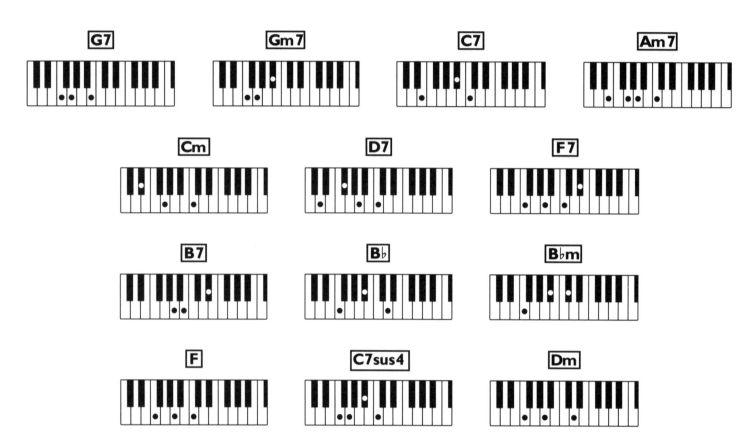

Voice: **Trumpet**

Rhythm: **Swing**

Tempo: ♩ = 120

You may va - ca - tion in Ha - wa - ii⸻

or go to Swit - zer - land to ski.⸻ When you're

scan - ning the snow cov - ered moun - tains ____ or fan - ning your - self by the sea, ____

don't dream of a - ny - bo - dy but me. ____

No mat - ter where you care to tra - vel, ____

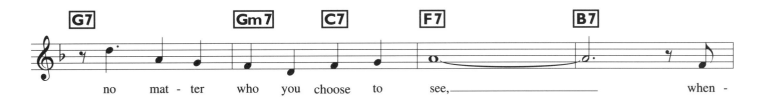

no mat - ter who you choose to see, ____ when -

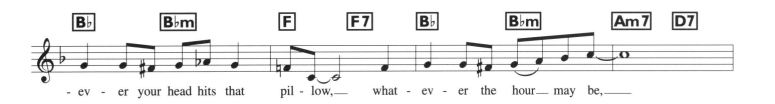

- ev - er your head hits that pil - low, ____ what - ev - er the hour ____ may be, ____

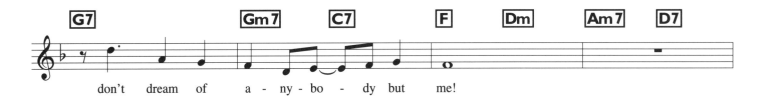

don't dream of a - ny - bo - dy but me!

Don't dream of a - ny - bo - dy but me. ____

FLY ME TO THE MOON
(In Other Words)

Words & Music by Bart Howard

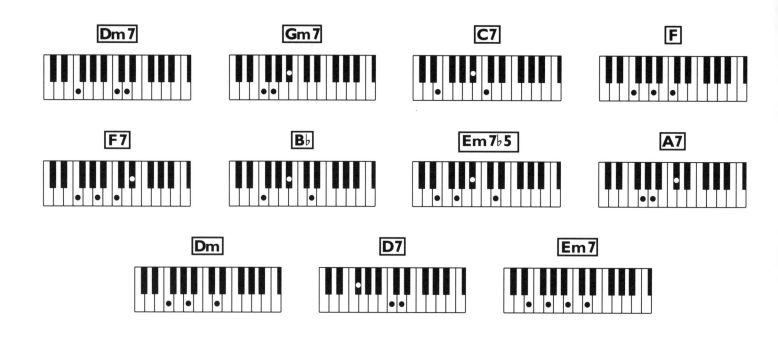

Voice: **Saxophone**

Rhythm: **2 beat**

Tempo: ♩ = 112

Fly me to the moon_____ and let me

play a - mong the stars._____ Let me see what spring-

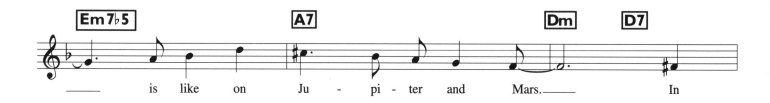

_____ is like on Ju - pi - ter and Mars._____ In

oth - er words_____ hold my hand!_____ In

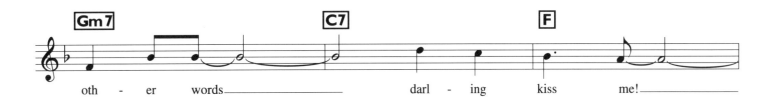

oth - er words_____ darl - ing kiss me!_____

_____ Fill my heart with song_____ and let me

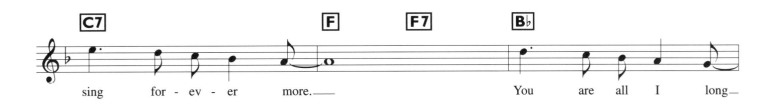

sing for - ev - er more.__ You are all I long__

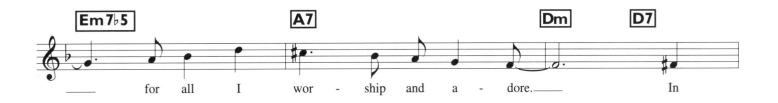

____ for all I wor - ship and a - dore.__ In

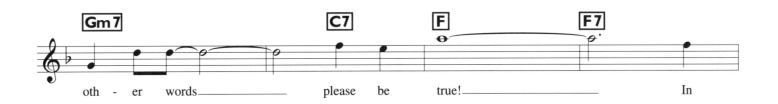

oth - er words_____ please be true!_____ In

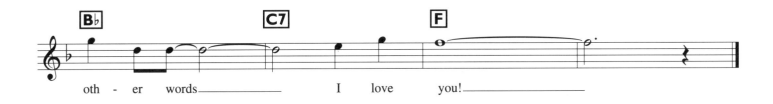

oth - er words_____ I love you!_____

FOR DANCERS ONLY

Music by Sy Oliver
Words by Don Raye & Vic Schoen
© Copyright 1939 MCA Music Corporation, USA.
MCA Music Limited, 77 Fulham Palace Road, London W6.
All Rights Reserved. International Copyright Secured.

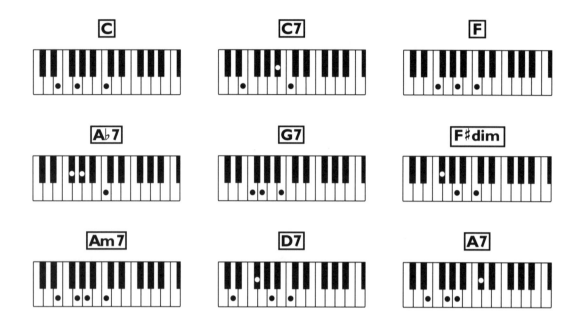

Voice: **Clarinet**

Rhythm: **Cool**

Tempo: ♩ = 126

Danc-ers, please lis-ten to me___ while I sing___ you a song___

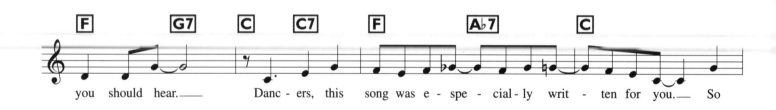

you should hear.___ Danc-ers, this song was e-spe-cial-ly writ-ten for you.___ So

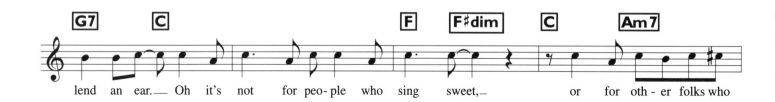

lend an ear.___ Oh it's not for peo-ple who sing sweet,___ or for oth-er folks who

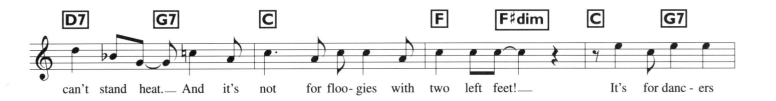

can't stand heat.— And it's not for floo-gies with two left feet!— It's for danc-ers

on - ly.— Oh it's not for old folks who aren't hep.— Or for peo-ple who have

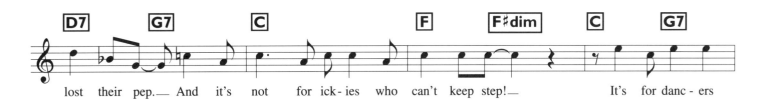

lost their pep.— And it's not for ick-ies who can't keep step!— It's for danc-ers

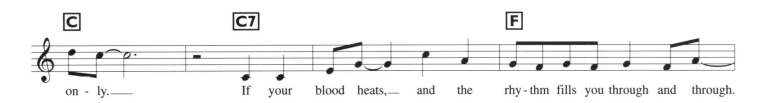

on - ly.— If your blood heats,— and the rhy-thm fills you through and through.

— If your heart beats,— bop de bop—you'll know this song's for you.— So if

you're a danc-er, there's no doubt,— you'll know what this song is all a-bout,— if you

don't you bet - ter sit this one out!— It's for danc - ers on - ly.—

HONEYSUCKLE ROSE

Music by Thomas 'Fats' Waller
Words by Andy Razaf
© Copyright 1929 Joy Music Incorporated, USA.
Campbell Connelly & Company Limited, 8/9 Frith Street, London W1 (50%)/
Redwood Music Limited, Iron Bridge House, 3 Bridge Approach, London N1 (50%)
for the Commonwealth of Nations, Germany, Austria, Switzerland, South Africa and Spain.
All Rights Reserved. International Copyright Secured.

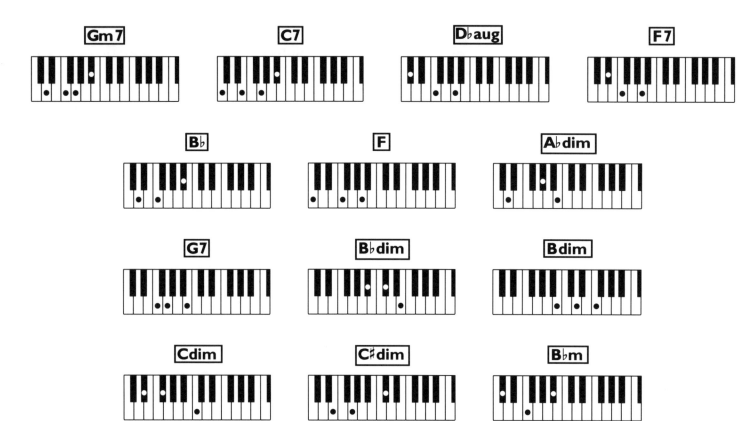

Voice: **Trumpet**

Rhythm: **2 beat**

Tempo: ♩ = **92**

Ev - 'ry hon - ey bee   fills with jea - lous - y   when they see you out with

me,   I   don't blame them   good - ness   knows,_____   hon - ey - suck - le

rose._____ When you're pass - ing by flow - ers droop and sigh,

and I know the rea - son why, you're much sweet - er good - ness knows,_____

____ hon - ey - suck - le rose._____ Don't buy su - gar,

you just__ have to touch my cup.__ You're my su - gar,

it's sweet__ when you stir it up.__ When I'm ta - kin' sips

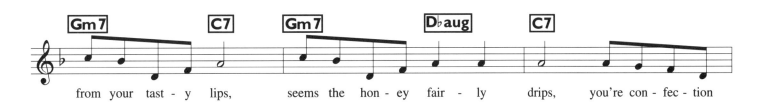

from your tast - y lips, seems the hon - ey fair - ly drips, you're con - fec - tion

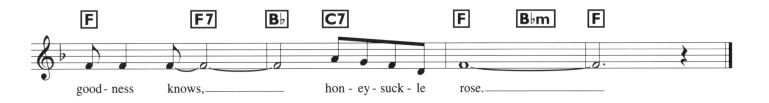

good - ness knows,_____ hon - ey - suck - le rose._____

I'M BEGINNING TO SEE THE LIGHT

Words & Music by Harry James, Duke Ellington, Johnny Hodges & Don George

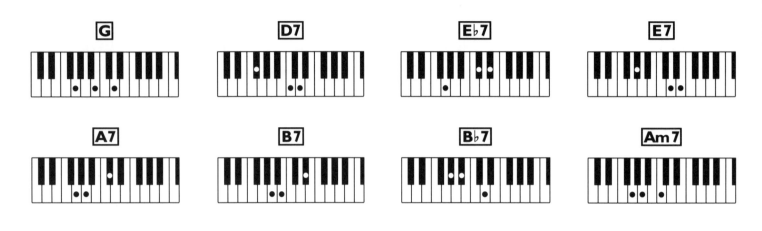

Voice: **Clarinet**

Rhythm: **Swing**

Tempo: ♩ = 108

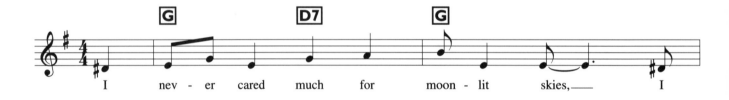

I nev - er cared much for moon - lit skies,—— I

nev - er wink back at fire - flies,—— but now that the stars are

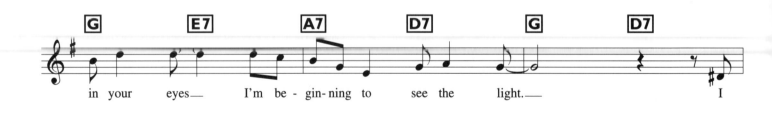

in your eyes—— I'm be - gin - ning to see the light.—— I

nev - er went in for af - ter - glow,—— or can - dle - light on the

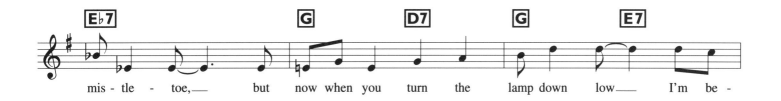

mis - tle - toe,___ but now when you turn the lamp down low___ I'm be -

- gin - ning to see the light.___ Used to ram - ble

through the park,___ sha - dow box - ing in the dark.___

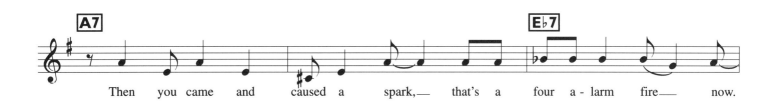

Then you came and caused a spark,___ that's a four a - larm fire___ now.

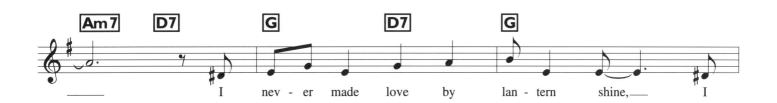

___ I nev - er made love by lan - tern shine,___ I

nev - er saw rain - bows in my wine,___ but now that your lips are

burn - ing mine,___ I'm be - gin - ning to see the light.___

IN A SENTIMENTAL MOOD

Words & Music by Duke Ellington, Irving Mills & Manny Kurtz

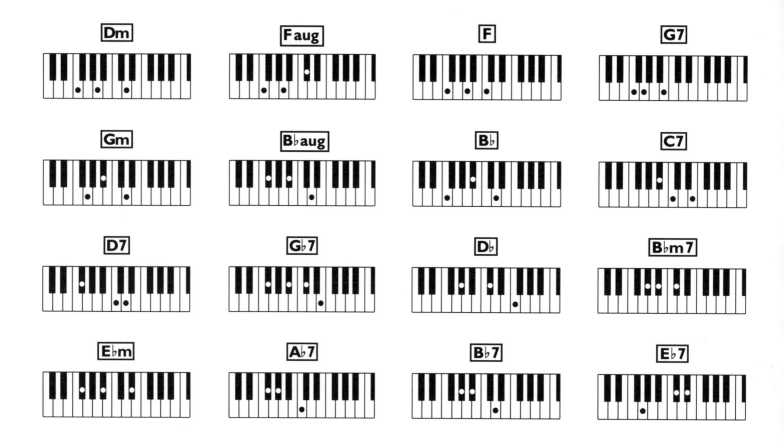

Voice: **Saxophone**

Rhythm: **2 beat**

Tempo: ♩ = 92

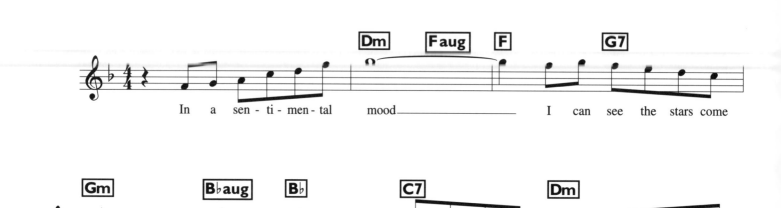

flame that lights the gloom. On the wings of ev-'ry kiss____

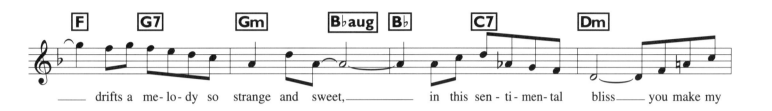

____ drifts a me-lo-dy so strange and sweet,____ in this sen-ti-men-tal bliss____ you make my

pa - ra - dise com - plete. Rose pe-tals seem to fall, it's

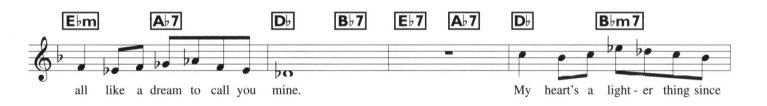

all like a dream to call you mine. My heart's a light-er thing since

you made this night a thing di - vine. In a sen-ti-men-tal mood____

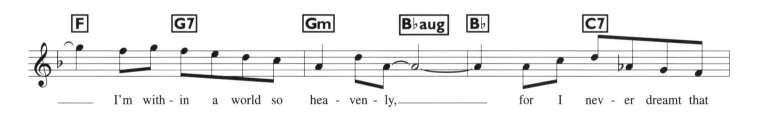

____ I'm with-in a world so hea-ven-ly,____ for I nev-er dreamt that

you'd____ be lov-ing sen - ti - men - tal me.

MEDITATION
(Meditaçao)

Original Words by Newton Mendonca
English Lyric by Norman Gimbel
Music by Antonio Carlos Jobim

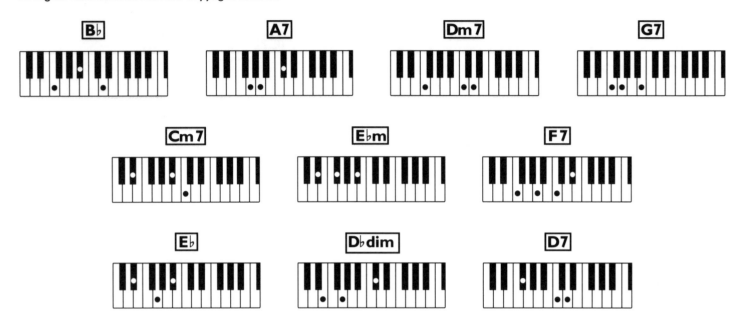

Voice: **Trumpet**

Rhythm: **Bossa Nova**

Tempo: ♩ = 84

In _____ my lon - li - ness, _____ when you've gone and I'm all

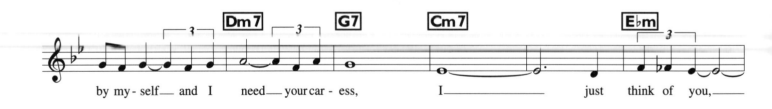

by my - self ___ and I need ___ your car - ess, I _____ just think of you, _____

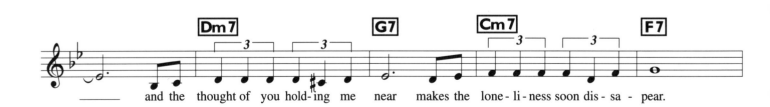

_____ and the thought of you hold - ing me near makes the lone - li - ness soon dis - sa - pear.

Though   you're far a - way,   I have on - ly to close my

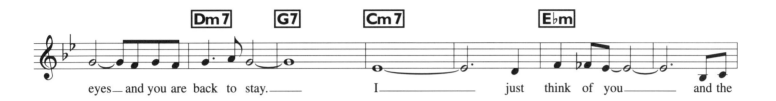

eyes and you are back to stay.   I   just think of you   and the

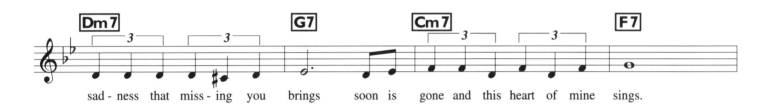

sad - ness that miss - ing you brings soon is gone and this heart of mine sings.

Yes   I love you so   and that for me is all I need to know.

I   will wait for you   'til the sun falls from out of the

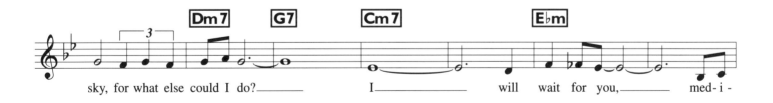

sky, for what else could I do?   I   will wait for you,   med - i -

-ta - ting how sweet life will be when you come back to me.

MOANIN'

Words by Jon Hendricks
Music by Bobby Timmons

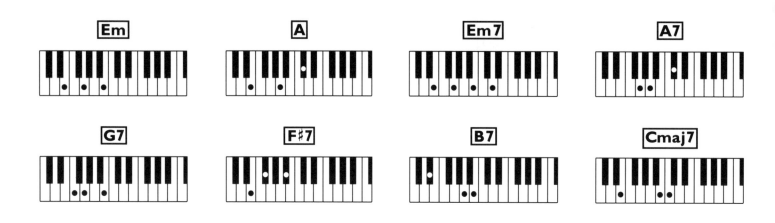

Voice: **Clarinet**

Rhythm: **2 beat**

Tempo: ♩ **= 88**

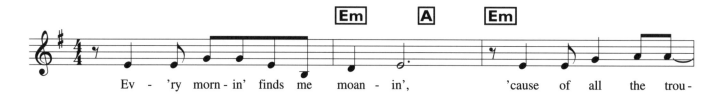

Ev - 'ry morn - in' finds me moan - in', 'cause of all the trou-

- ble I see.___ Life's a los - in' gam - ble to me,___

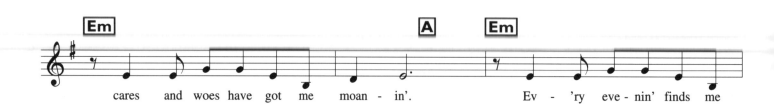

cares and woes have got me moan - in'. Ev - 'ry eve - nin' finds me

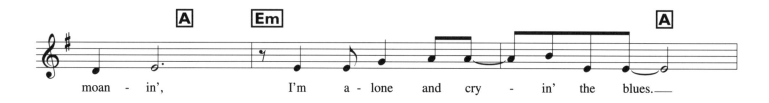

moan - in', I'm a - lone and cry - in' the blues.___

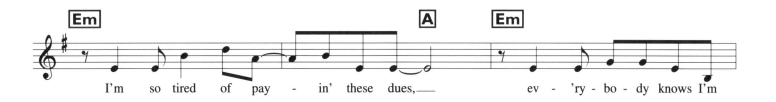

I'm so tired of pay - in' these dues,___ ev - 'ry - bo - dy knows I'm

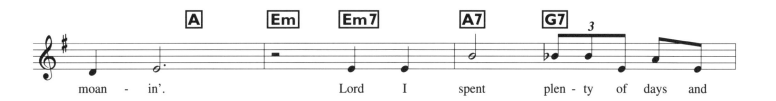

moan - in'. Lord I spent plen - ty of days and

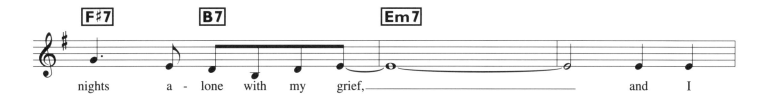

nights a - lone with my grief,_____ and I

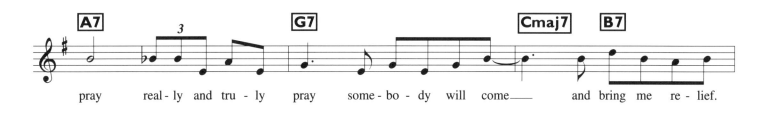

pray real - ly and tru - ly pray some - bo - dy will come___ and bring me re - lief.

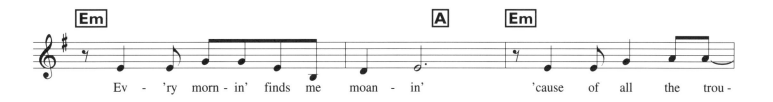

Ev - 'ry morn - in' finds me moan - in' 'cause of all the trou -

- bles I see.___ Life's a los - in' gam - ble to me,___

cares and woes have got me moan - in'.___

SATIN DOLL

Words by Johnny Mercer
Music by Duke Ellington & Billy Strayhorn
© Copyright 1953 & 1960 by Tempo Music Incorporated, USA.
Campbell Connelly & Company Limited, 8/9 Frith Street, London W1.
All Rights Reserved. International Copyright Secured.

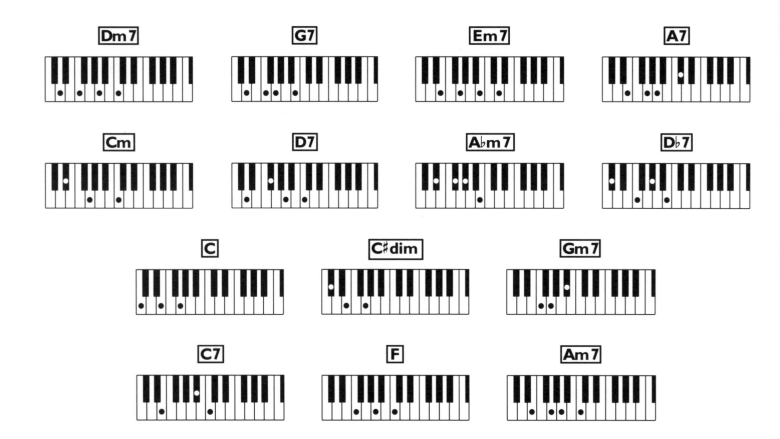

Voice: **Clarinet**

Rhythm: **2 beat**

Tempo: ♩ = 104

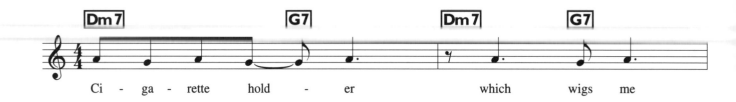

Ci - ga - rette hold - er   which   wigs   me

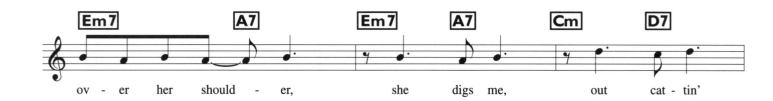

ov - er her should - er,   she   digs me,   out   cat - tin'

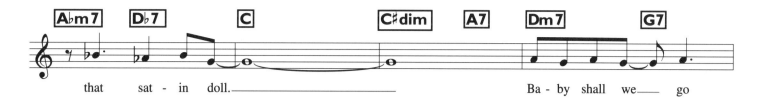

that sat - in doll._____ Ba - by shall we__ go

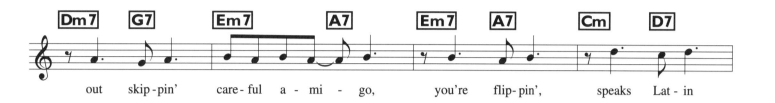

out skip-pin' care-ful a - mi - go, you're flip-pin', speaks Lat - in

that sat - in doll._____ She's no - bo - dy's fool, so I'm

play - ing it cool as can be._____ I'll give it a whirl__ but I

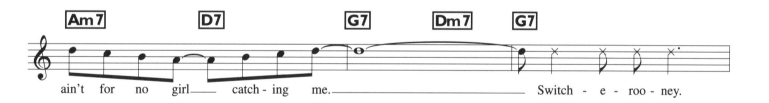

ain't for no girl__ catch - ing me._____ Switch - e - roo - ney.

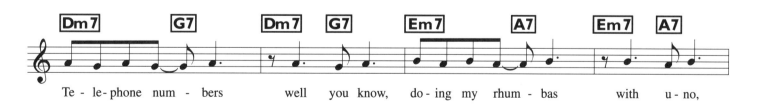

Te - le - phone num - bers well you know, do - ing my rhum - bas with u - no,

and that 'n' my sat - in doll._____

SLIGHTLY OUT OF TUNE
(Desafinado)

English Lyric by Jon Hendricks & Jessie Cavanaugh
Music by Antonio Carlos Jobim

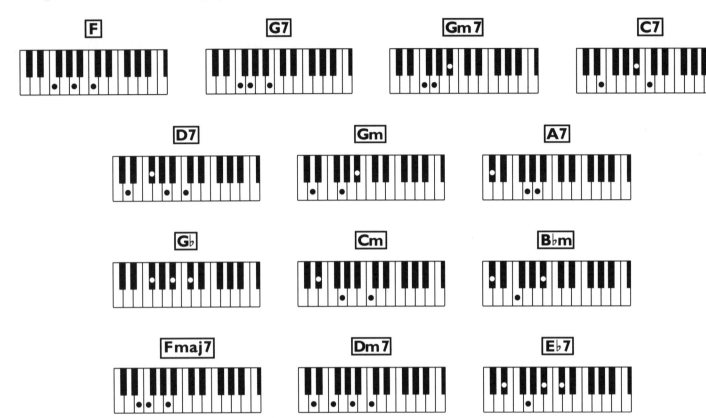

Voice: **Trumpet**

Rhythm: **Beguine**

Tempo: ♩ = 116

Love is like a nev - er end - ing me - lo - dy.____

Po - ets have com - pared it to a sym - pho - ny.____

A sym-pho-ny con-duc - ted by the light-ing of the moon.

But our song of love is slight-ly out of tune.

Tune your heart to mine the way it used to be.

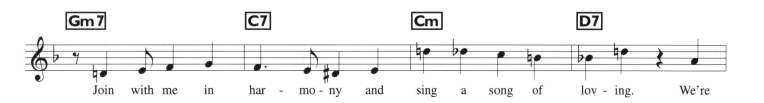

Join with me in har - mo-ny and sing a song of lov - ing. We're

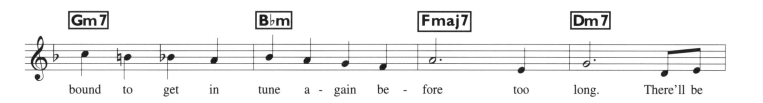

bound to get in tune a - gain be - fore too long. There'll be

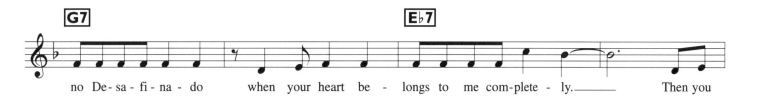

no De- sa- fi- na- do when your heart be - longs to me com-plete - ly. Then you

won't be slight- ly out of tune, you'll sing a - long with me.

SOLITUDE

Words by Eddie de Lange & Irving Mills
Music by Duke Ellington

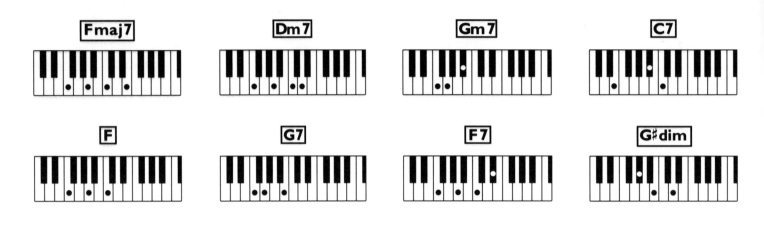

Voice: **Vibraphone**

Rhythm: **2 beat**

Tempo: ♩ = 108

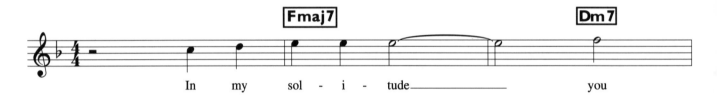

In my sol - i - tude_____ you

haunt   me   with   re - ver - ies_____

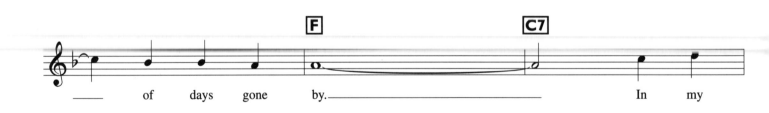

_____ of days gone by._____ In my

sol - i - tude_____ you   taunt

me with mem - o - ries _____ that nev - er

die. _____ I sit in my chair, I'm

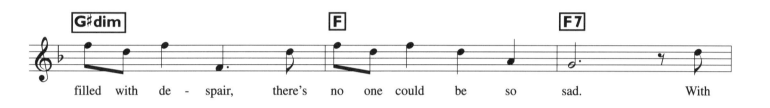

filled with de - spair, there's no one could be so sad. With

gloom ev - 'ry - where, I sit and I stare, I know that I'll soon go

mad. In my sol - i - tude _____ I'm

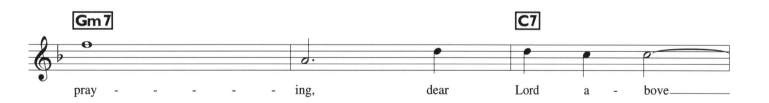

pray - - - - - ing, dear Lord a - bove _____

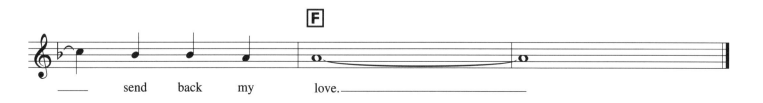

_____ send back my love. _____

SWEET SUE – JUST YOU

Words by Will J. Harris
Music by Victor Young

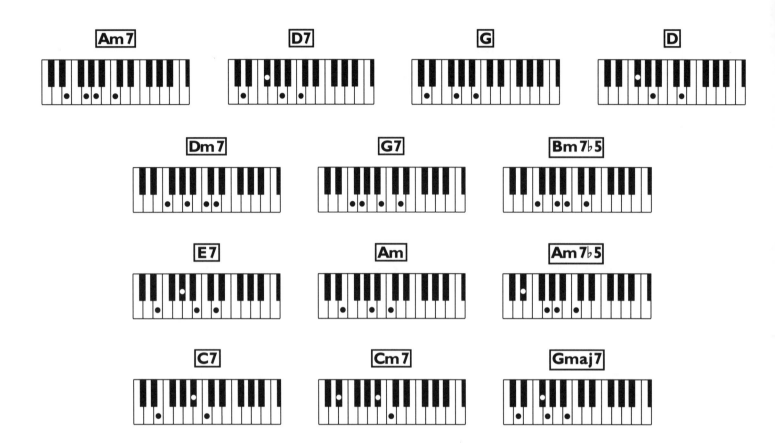

Voice: **Trumpet**

Rhythm: **2 beat**

Tempo: ♩ = 126

Ev - 'ry star a - bove_____ knows the

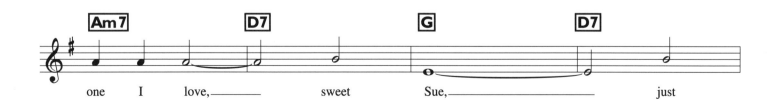

one I love,_____ sweet Sue,_____ just

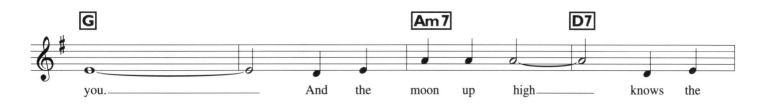

you._____ And the moon up high_____ knows the

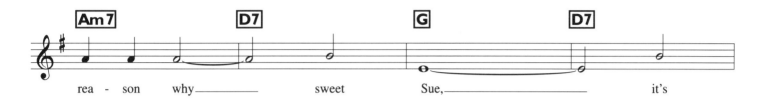

rea - son why_____ sweet Sue,_____ it's

you._____ No one else it seems_____ ev - er

shares my dreams_____ and with - out you, dear, I

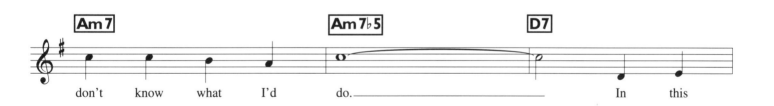

don't know what I'd do._____ In this

heart of mine_____ you live all the time_____ sweet

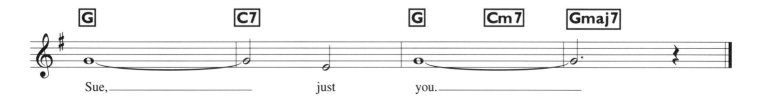

Sue,_____ just you._____

TAKE THE 'A' TRAIN

Words & Music by Billy Strayhorn

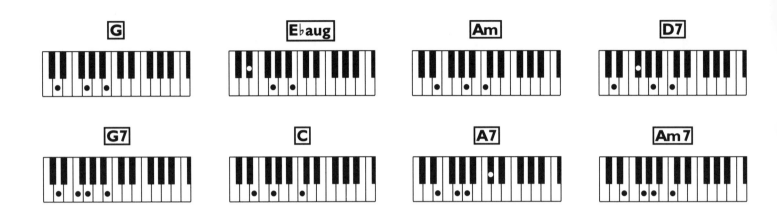

Voice: **Saxophone**

Rhythm: **Cool**

Tempo: ♩ = 108

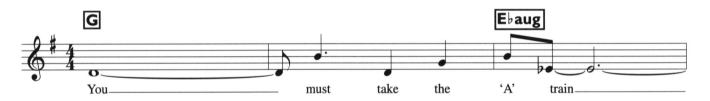

You _____ must take the 'A' train _____

_____ to go to Su - gar Hill way up in

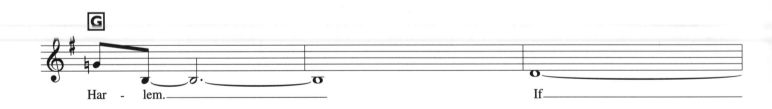

Har - lem. _____ If _____

_____ you miss the 'A' train, _____

you'll find you've missed the quick - est way to

Har - lem. Hur - ry,

get on now it's com - ing.

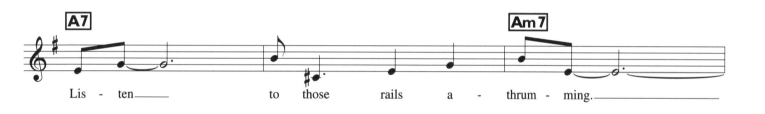
Lis - ten to those rails a - thrum - ming.

All 'board! get on the

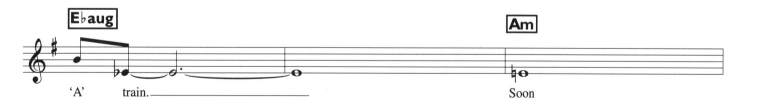
'A' train. Soon

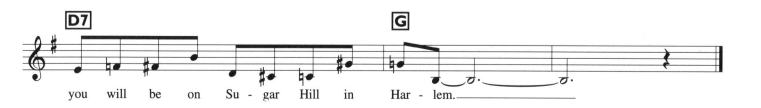
you will be on Su - gar Hill in Har - lem.

TIME'S A-WASTIN'

Words & Music by Duke Ellington, Mercer Ellington & Don George

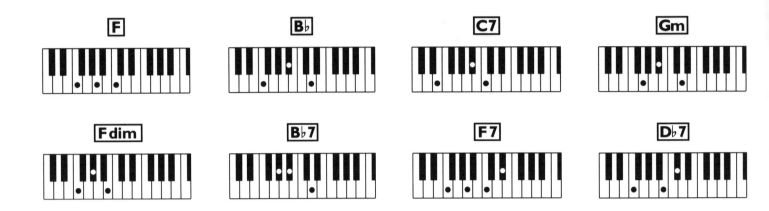

Voice: **Saxophone**

Rhythm: **Cool**

Tempo: ♩ = 88

Lis - ten ba - by the times a - wast - - - in', ____

an' I'm tel - lin' ya it's dis - grace - - - in'. ____

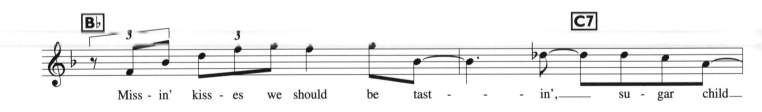

Miss - in' kiss - es we should be tast - - - in', ____ su - gar child

____ now I'm beg - gin' your lips to hast - - - en. ____ I

need 'em so_____ 'cause I got a feel-in' I got a glow._

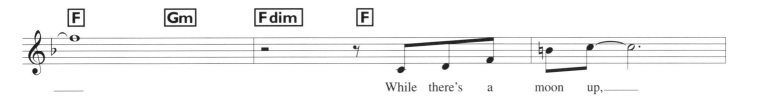

_____ While there's a moon up,_____

can't our song be more than just a tune up?_____

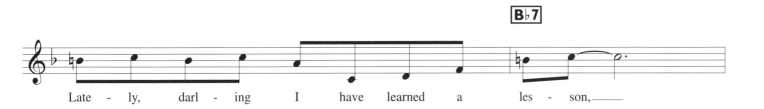

Late - ly, darl - ing I have learned a les - son,_____

more than just my dreams de - sire ca - ress - in'._ So hast - en now_ 'cause

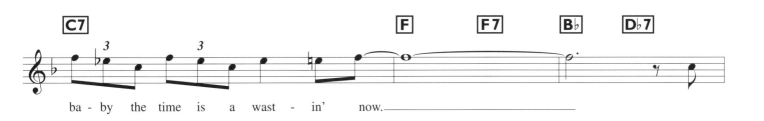

ba - by the time is a wast - in' now._____

TUXEDO JUNCTION

Words by Buddy Feyne
Music by Erskine Hawkins, William Johnson & Julian Dash

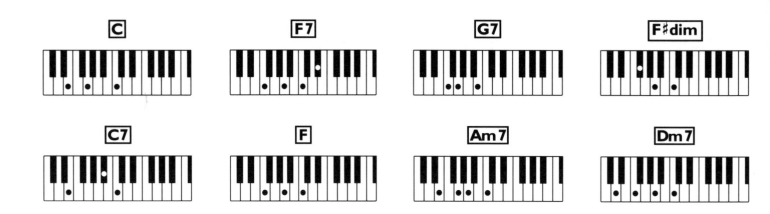

Voice: **Saxophone**

Rhythm: **Swing**

Tempo: ♩ = 112

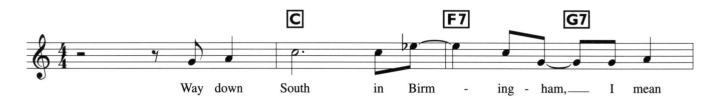

Way down South in Birm - ing - ham,— I mean

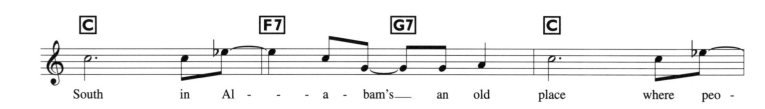

South in Al - - - a - bam's— an old place where peo -

- ple go— to dance— the night— a - way.— They all

drive or walk— for miles— to get jive that South -

- ern style,— s - low jive that makes— you want— to dance—

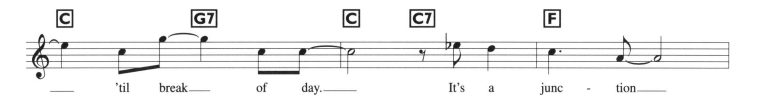
— 'til break— of day.— It's a junc - tion—

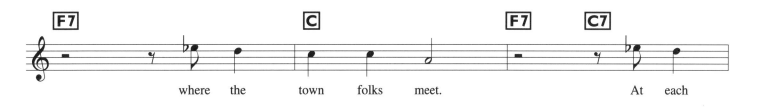
where the town folks meet. At each

func - tion— in their tux they— greet—

— you.— Come on down, for - get— your care.— Come on

down, you'll find— me there.— So long town! I'm head -

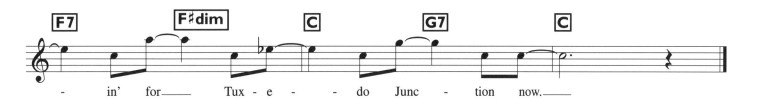
- in' for— Tux - e - do Junc - tion now.—

UNDECIDED

Words by Sid Robin
Music by Charles Shavers

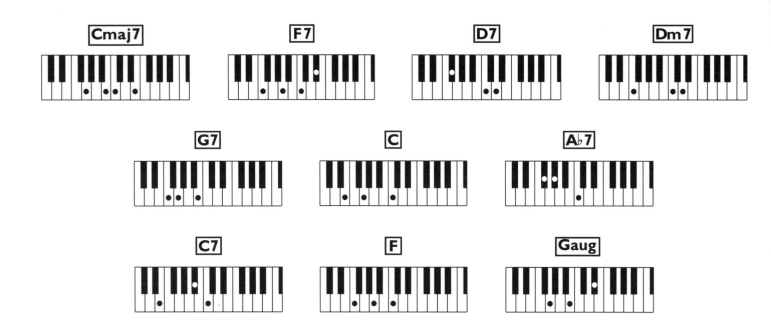

Voice: **Jazz Organ**

Rhythm: **2 beat**

Tempo: ♩ = 100

First you say you do and then you don't,___ and then you say you will and

then you won't.___ You're un-de-ci-ded now, so what are you gon-na do?

___ Now you want to play, and then it's no,___ and

F7 ... **D7**

when you say you'll stay, that's when you go.___ You're un - de - ci - ded now, so

Dm7 ... **G7** ... **C**

what are you gon - na do?___ I've been

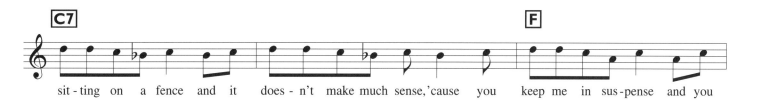

C7 ... **F**

sit - ting on a fence and it does - n't make much sense, 'cause you keep me in sus - pense and you

D7

know it.___ Then you pro - mise to re - turn. When you don't I real - ly burn. Well, I

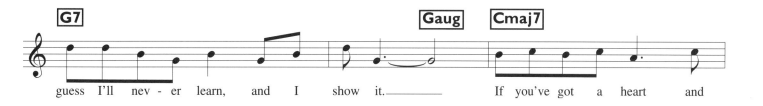

G7 ... **Gaug** **Cmaj7**

guess I'll nev - er learn, and I show it.___ If you've got a heart and

F7

if you're kind,___ then don't keep us a - part. Make up your mind.___ You're

D7 ... **Dm7** **G7** **C**

un - de - ci - ded now, so what are you gon - na do.___

VIOLETS FOR YOUR FURS

Words by Tom Adair
Music by Matt Dennis

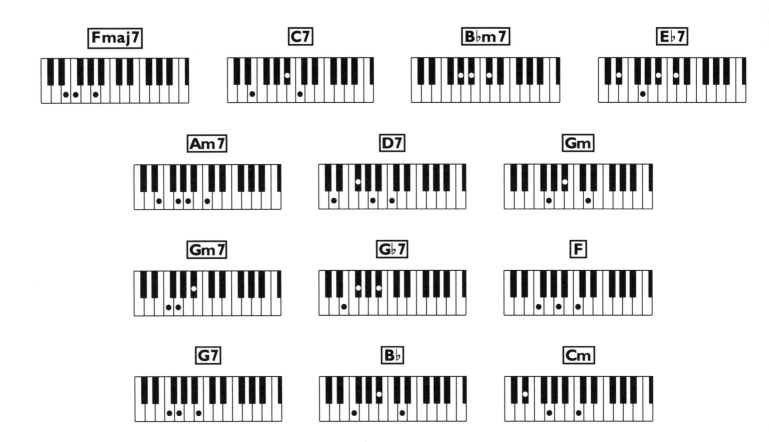

Voice: **Jazz Organ**

Rhythm: **2 beat**

Tempo: ♩ **= 84**

I bought you vi - o - lets for your furs___ and it was Spring for a while, re -

- mem - ber?___ I bought you vi - o - lets for your furs___ and there was

April in that De - cem - ber.___ The snow drift - ed down on the flow - ers___ and

melt - ed where it lay. The snow looked like dew in the blos - soms___ as

on a sum - mer day. I bought you vi - o - lets for your furs___ and there was

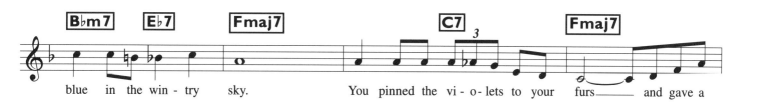

blue in the win - try sky. You pinned the vi - o - lets to your furs___ and gave a

lift to the crowds pass - ing by. You smiled at me so sweet - ly, since

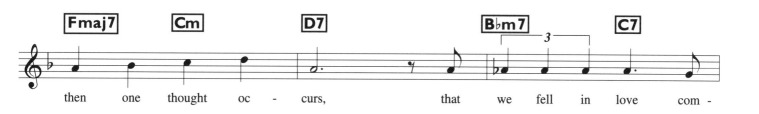

then one thought oc - curs, that we fell in love com -

- plete - ly the day that I bought you vi - o - lets for your furs.

EASIEST KEYBOARD COLLECTION

Easy-to-play melody line arrangements for all keyboards with chord symbols and lyrics. Suggested registration, rhythm and tempo are included for each song together with keyboard diagrams showing left-hand chord voicings used.

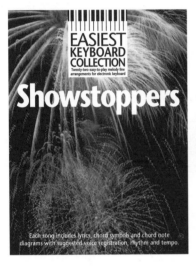

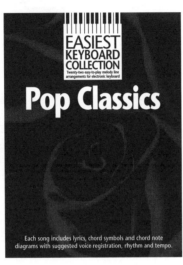

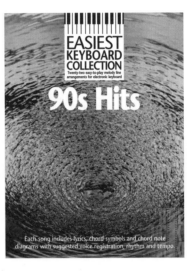

Showstoppers
Consider Yourself (Oliver!), Do You Hear The People Sing? (Les Misérables), I Know Him So Well (Chess), Maria (West Side Story), Smoke Gets In Your Eyes (Roberta) and 17 more big stage hits.
Order No. AM944218

Pop Classics
A Whiter Shade Of Pale (Procol Harum), Bridge Over Troubled Water (Simon & Garfunkel), Crocodile Rock (Elton John) and nineteen more classic pop hits, including Hey Jude (The Beatles), Imagine (John Lennon), Massachusetts (The Bee Gees) and Stars (Simply Red).
Order No. AM944196

90s Hits
Over twenty of the greatest hits of the 1990s, including Always (Bon Jovi), Fields Of Gold (Sting), Have I Told You Lately (Rod Stewart), One Sweet Day (Mariah Carey), Say You'll Be There (Spice Girls), and Wonderwall (Oasis).
Order No. AM944229

TV Themes
Twenty-two great themes from popular TV series, including Casualty, EastEnders, Gladiators, Heartbeat, I'm Always Here (Baywatch), Red Dwarf and The Black Adder.
Order No. AM944207

Also available...

Film Themes, Order No. AM952050 **Chart Hits**, Order No. AM952083
Jazz Classics, Order No. AM952061 **Classical Themes**, Order No. AM952094
Classic Blues, Order No. AM950697 **Christmas**, Order No. AM952105
Love Songs, Order No. AM950708 **Ballads**, Order No. AM952116
Pop Hits, Order No. AM952072 **Broadway**, Order No. AM952127